The Pug who wanted to be a Mermaid

Bella Swift

Contents

Chapter One

Peggy the pug was flopped under the big oak tree in the back garden, panting in the shade. It was *soooo* hot! On summer days like today, she wished her short, tan-coloured fur wasn't quite so warm and cosy. A fly buzzed around her nose, but Peggy couldn't be bothered to swat it away with her paw. She lolled on the grass and thought about cold things, like the kitchen floor tiles . . . snow . . . and ICE CREAM!

"Peggy!" someone called from the house, interrupting her vanilla-flavoured daydream.

Hearing her friend Chloe's voice, Peggy sat up and wagged her curly little tail. She always had energy to play with her best friend!

Chloe and her little sister, Ruby, came running over, flushed and sweaty.

"Guess what!" said Chloe, crouching down to stroke Peggy. "School's out! It's the summer holidays!"

"No more homework until September!" sang Ruby, doing a cartwheel on the grass.

"Yippee!" barked Peggy excitedly. She would see more of Chloe and Ruby – and their big brother Finn – over the summer holidays. She missed the kids when they were at school.

Dad came out, holding a big sheet of black card with brightly coloured balls of different sizes glued to it. "How was your last day of school?" he asked the girls.

"Fun!" said Ruby. "We got extra playtime and I got a certificate for being a Super Helper."

"Well done," said Dad. "By the way

9

– what is this thing? I found it in the kitchen."

"Oh, that's my solar system project," said Chloe. "I made it in science class this term. My teacher said I could take it home."

"Oh," said Dad. "It's . . . very big."

"Not compared to a planet," said Chloe. "Did you know that Neptune is four times the size of Earth?"

"Is that so?" said Dad. "Well, this was certainly taking up most of the kitchen table."

"I'll keep it in my bedroom," said Chloe, taking her solar system off Dad. "Is it OK if I go to the park? Everyone from school is meeting up there."

"Can I come too?" pleaded Ruby.

"And me!" said Peggy, but to the humans it just sounded like barking.

"Sure," said Dad. "Finn just texted to say he's hanging out at the park with some friends. I'll ask him to keep an eye on you."

Chloe took her solar system project up to her bedroom. Then she packed a bag with some snacks, clipped on Peggy's lead and they headed to the park. The pavement felt hot against Peggy's paws as she trotted along by Chloe's side.

"Look! There's Finn!" said Ruby as they went through the park gates.

She waved to her big brother, who
was kicking a football around on the
grass with his friend Zach. Peggy tried
to chase after the football, but Chloe
tugged on her lead. "This way, Peggy.
I'm meeting Ellie and Hannah."

Ruby spotted some of her friends
from her Reception class in the
playground and ran over to join them
on the roundabout. Just looking at them

spinning around made Peggy feel dizzy!

Chloe's friends were sitting on the grass near the playground, making daisy chains. Peggy was delighted to see that Hannah had brought her little terrier, Princess, along.

"Hi, Peggy!" yapped Princess. She had a yellow bow in her fur that matched Hannah's sundress perfectly.

As the two little dogs sniffed each other happily, Chloe sat down with her friends.

"I'm so glad it's the summer holidays," said Hannah, putting her daisy chain around Princess's neck.

"Me too," said Ellie. "My family's going camping for two weeks. We're sleeping in a tent and hiking every day. At night, we're going to roast marshmallows on the camp fire."

"That sounds fun," said Hannah, fanning herself with her sunhat. "I'm going on holiday to Spain. We're staying in a hotel that has two pools – one of them even has a water slide."

"Oooh!" said Chloe. "That's so cool." She frowned. "But what about Princess? Can she go on the plane with you?"

"Princess is going to stay in a kennel while we're away," said Hannah, stroking her dog's head. "She really loves it there, with all the other dogs. It's just like a holiday for her, too."

Princess groaned and rolled her eyes. "I hate it at that kennel," she told Peggy. "It's awful – I have to sleep in a cage, and all the other dogs are constantly barking."

Peggy felt sorry for her friend. A kennel sounded a lot like a dog shelter. She had been in one of those before Chloe and her family adopted her. She'd never felt so scared and lonely.

"At least it's only for two weeks," Peggy said, trying to reassure her. "You know Hannah will come back for you."

"Where are you going on holiday, Chloe?" asked Hannah.

Chloe shrugged. "I don't think we're

going anywhere this year. My mum's been so busy setting up her café."

Chloe's mum ran a café called Pups and Cups, where people could bring their dogs and buy tasty treats – for dogs and humans.

"That's too bad," said Ellie. "But at least you always get lots of yummy snacks from the café."

"True . . ." said Chloe, reaching into her bag and taking out a plastic container of chocolate chip cookies which she shared with her friends.

"Hey," yapped Princess. "What about us?"

Peggy whined hopefully and Chloe

took out another
container. She
gave Peggy and
Princess each
a bacon and
peanut butter-
flavoured dog
biscuit shaped like
a bone.

They stayed in the park until the sun
began to set, then Finn rounded up his
sisters.

"Tomorrow I'm going to have a long
lie-in," he said, bouncing his football up
and down as they walked home.

A lie-in sounded good to Peggy.

She was exhausted after playing with Princess.

As they came up the front path, Mum was just getting home from the café. "Hi," she said. "I ordered pizza. It's too hot to cook today."

When the pizzas arrived, Peggy's family sat down at the table and tucked into their dinner.

"I love pizza!" said Ruby, biting into a slice and getting tomato sauce all over her face.

"Zach is going on holiday to Italy with his parents," said Finn. "I bet he'll eat pizza every single day."

"I wish we were going on holiday,"

said Chloe, sighing as she picked a
mushroom off her slice of pizza.

Mum and Dad exchanged looks.
"Actually," said Mum, grinning, "we
have some good news. The café's been
doing pretty well, so we're going to the
seaside for a week."

The children stared at their parents in
disbelief.

"No way!" shouted Finn. Chloe and
Ruby shrieked with excitement. It was
so loud Peggy had to cover her ears with
her paws!

"We're staying in a place called
Mermaid Cottage," said Dad, showing
them a picture on his phone. "It has three

bedrooms and it's right by the beach."

Chloe's eyes widened as she looked at the screen. "It's so cute," she said.

"I can't wait for a break," said Mum. "I'm going to lie on the beach and read in the sunshine."

"Not me," said Ruby. "I'm going to build sandcastles."

"Do you think we could go deep

sea fishing?" asked Finn.

Dad nodded. "Definitely."

"I'm going to go swimming every day," said Chloe. Then she added, "And maybe I'll even get to see a mermaid."

Everyone was excited about the holiday – except Peggy. Would she have to stay in a dog kennel like Princess?

"Wait a minute," said Chloe, as if she'd read her mind. "Who will look after Peggy?"

"We will," said Mum. "She's coming with us, of course."

"Did you hear that, Pegs?" asked Chloe, scooping Peggy on to her lap. "You're going on holiday!"

Peggy gave a bark of joy and wagged her tail. She'd never been to the seaside before and she couldn't wait!

Chapter Two

"Just one more sleep until we go on holiday!" announced Chloe, marking an X on the kitchen calendar. The children had been busy for the first few weeks of the summer holidays. Finn had gone to music camp, Chloe had tennis lessons with her friends and Ruby was taking a swimming class at the local leisure centre. She'd just come back from the pool, and her curly hair was still damp.

"I swam underwater today," Ruby said proudly. "My teacher called me a little mermaid."

"Ooh! *The Little Mermaid*," said Chloe. "Let's watch it again."

The girls helped themselves to fruity ice lollies from the freezer, then went into the living room and switched on the television. Peggy sat between them and watched the film too. She liked it because there were lots of funny sea creatures in it, like crabs and seagulls.

I wonder if I'll make any new animal

friends on holiday, she thought hopefully.

When their favourite song came on, the girls jumped off the sofa and started dancing around the living room.

"Under the sea!" sang Chloe, twirling her sister around.

"Under the sea!" chorused Ruby.

They knew all the words. So did Peggy. She joined in, howling along to the music.

When the film was over, Finn came in. "I can't believe you watched that stupid old movie again," he said. "You've seen it a million times already."

"We might see a mermaid on holiday," Ruby told Finn.

"Yeah right," he scoffed. "Mermaids aren't real."

Chloe stuck her tongue out at her brother. "Just because you've never seen one, doesn't mean they don't exist."

"Let's watch something decent," Finn said, grabbing the remote. Chloe tried to get it off him, but he held it up over her head and switched over to a documentary about sharks.

"Awesome," said Finn, as an enormous Great White shark swam across the screen, its jaws open to reveal rows of sharp teeth. "Maybe we'll see one of these on holiday."

Peggy whimpered and covered her eyes with her paws as the shark attacked a school of fish.

"Maybe one will eat you," said Chloe grumpily.

Ruby's eyes widened in fear. "Are there really sharks at the seaside?"

"Don't worry, Rubes," said Finn,

tousling her hair. "There aren't any Great Whites where we're going. Just little sharks."

That didn't make Peggy feel very reassured. She was only little – even a small shark could probably eat her in one bite!

Everyone was too excited to eat much breakfast the next morning, even though Dad had cooked bacon and eggs to use up what was left in the fridge.

"I can't believe we're going on holiday today!" Chloe said, scraping her leftover breakfast into Peggy's bowl.

"We've got lots to do before we leave," said Mum, handing everyone a packing list.

"I'd better get Coco's things together," said Chloe. "Ellie's coming to collect her soon."

Chloe's friend Ellie was looking after Coco the bunny, while the rest of the family was at the seaside. Peggy followed Chloe outside to the back garden. As she got a bag of wood shavings, a travel carrier and some rabbit food out of the shed, Peggy went over to the rabbit hutch to chat with Coco.

"Hi, Peggy," said the black-and-white rabbit. "Are you excited about your holiday? I bet you'll have lots of fun."

Peggy nodded. "I'm sorry you can't come with us, though."

"Don't worry," said Coco, her whiskers twitching. "I can't wait to see my mum again. We've got so much to catch up on. It will be great."

Coco's mum was Daisy, Ellie's pet rabbit. Peggy was relieved to hear that Coco was looking forward to her holiday, too!

When Ellie arrived, Chloe took Coco out of her hutch and gave her one last cuddle. Then she put the bunny into the travel carrier.

"I'll take really good care of her," promised Ellie.

"I know you will," said Chloe, smiling.

"Send me some pics," said Ellie.

"I will," said Chloe.

"Have fun with Daisy!" Peggy barked.

Once Ellie had taken Coco home, Chloe went upstairs to start packing. She opened her chest of drawers and started taking out shorts, socks and T-shirts,

throwing them into the suitcase on her
bed. A swimming
costume even
landed on
Peggy's head!

"Where
are they …"
muttered Chloe,
searching through
all her drawers. "Mum!" she
hollered down the stairs. "I can't find my
goggles!"

"Check the cupboard in the hall!"
Mum called back.

Stepping over Peggy, Chloe ran out of
the room to look for her goggles.

Peggy wandered into the hallway.

"Dad!" shouted Finn, bursting out of his room. "I can't find my fishing net!"

"It might be in the shed!" Dad called back to him.

Finn nearly trod on Peggy's paw as he hurried past.

"Help!" yelled Ruby, dragging a bulging backpack out of her room. She was holding a tatty stuffed elephant in one hand. "I can't fit Mr Flump into my backpack!"

"Excuse me, Peggy," said Mum, brushing past her as she came upstairs. She looked at Ruby's bag and shook her head. "You can't take all of these, sweetie." Mum began pulling cuddly toys from Ruby's bag. Peggy had to climb over a plush dinosaur and a stuffed lion to get by.

Dad dashed past, holding the hamper. "Clean clothes coming through," he said, nearly tripping over Peggy.

Everyone was rushing around, frantically packing. No matter where Peggy sat, she always seemed to be in the way.

I'd better lie low for a bit, she thought. Peggy went back into Chloe's room and squeezed under the bed. Nobody would step on her there! She shut her eyes, and soon dozed off.

When Peggy woke up, the house was
quiet.

Too quiet.

She wriggled out from under the bed
and looked around. *Where is everyone?*
Peggy wandered out into the hallway,
but there was no sign of anyone. And all
the suitcases were gone, too.

Starting to feel worried, Peggy went downstairs. But her family wasn't anywhere to be seen.

Maybe they're packing up the car, she thought.

Jumping up on the windowsill, she looked out at the driveway.

The car was gone.

They've gone on holiday without me!
she realised in dismay. "Oh no!" she
wailed. "They left me behind!" How
would she survive for a whole week on
her own?

Just then, a car sped down the road and
swerved into the driveway, stopping with
a loud squeal of brakes. Chloe jumped
out of the car, unlocked the front door
and ran inside.

"Peggy!" she cried.

Peggy ran to her friend and jumped
into her arms, wriggling with joy. She
licked Chloe's face all over. She had
never been so relieved to see anyone in
her entire life!

"I'm so sorry!" said Chloe. "We came back as soon as we realised we forgot to pack the most important thing of all . . ." Chloe gave Peggy a kiss. ". . . You!"

Chapter Three

"Are we almost there yet?" asked Chloe, tapping her mum's shoulder.

"Not much further to go," Mum said, without taking her eyes off the road.

"I need to do a wee," said Ruby, squirming next to Peggy in the back seat.

Me too, thought Peggy. They had been

driving for ages. It had been hours since they'd stopped for a picnic lunch at a rest area.

"Hold it in a bit longer," said Dad. "We're nearly there."

"Can we change the music?" moaned Finn. "If I have to listen to *The Little Mermaid* soundtrack one more time I'm going to scream."

Dad changed the music to a rock band, and Finn pretended he was drumming along.

"Cut it out!" whined Chloe, shoving her brother's elbow out of the way. "Get off my side."

Before an all-out war could break out

in the back seat, Dad turned around and said, "Look! You can see the sea in the distance."

Peggy stuck her head out of the window to get a better view. Her ears flapped as the wind rushed against her face. Along with the usual car scents of petrol and rubber, she could also smell something salty and a bit fishy in the air.

Mmmm, thought Peggy, sniffing.

"Left here," said Dad, and Mum steered the car off the motorway and on to a road leading down to the coast.

After passing through a few villages, they turned again, down a bumpy road. At the very end of it, Peggy could see something blue sparkling in the distance. The sea!

The road ended at a little bay with two small stone cottages. Beyond them, a wooden path wound through the dunes, leading down to a sandy beach.

"We're here!" cried Chloe.

Mum parked the car and everyone tumbled out.

Aaah, thought Peggy, stretching out

her hind legs. *That's better!*

"Which one is ours?" asked Ruby. One of the cottages was painted white and had wild roses climbing up the front. The other was grey and had colourful buoys and fishing nets piled up outside it.

"It must be this one," said Chloe, pointing to the white cottage. It had a little painted sign over the door that read *Mermaid Cottage*.

"The owner said it would be unlocked," said Mum.

"Me first!" cried Ruby, opening the door and running inside.

Peggy hurried in after her, with Chloe following right behind.

"Oh, it's adorable!" said Chloe, looking around, enchanted.

The living room was painted white, with blue curtains in the windows. In the middle was a wood-burning stove surrounded by worn but comfy-looking armchairs, and shelves stocked with books, board games, playing cards and jigsaw puzzles. On the dining table was a jug filled with roses, and their sweet scent filled the whole cottage.

"I could use a hand with the luggage," said Dad, staggering in with two heavy suitcases.

"I'll help," said Finn. He hurried outside to get more bags from the boot, while Peggy and the girls raced around, investigating.

The cottage had three bedrooms – one with a double bed for Mum and Dad, a tiny room with a single bed for Finn, and one with bunk beds for Chloe and Ruby.

"Mermaids!" gasped Chloe in delight. The girls' bedroom was decorated with mermaids everywhere. There were mermaids on the curtains, mermaids on the duvet covers and a painting of a mermaid on the wall.

"Bagsy the top bunk!" said Chloe.

"But I've never slept up high before," said Ruby, pouting.

"You're too little," said Chloe. "You

might fall out of bed in the night."

"No I won't," Ruby protested.

The girls glared at each other, their arms crossed, each unwilling to give in.

Peggy gazed up at the top bunk apprehensively. She usually slept in Chloe's bed, but there was no way her little legs could get up there! *I guess I'll have to sleep on the ground*, she thought sadly. She looked down at the floor and whimpered.

Chloe suddenly realised what was wrong. "OK," she said, sitting down on the bottom bunk and patting her thighs, so Peggy would jump on to her lap. "I guess you can have the top bunk, Ruby.

Peggy and I will sleep down here."

Thank goodness! thought Peggy, licking Chloe's face. She should have known her best friend would never let her down.

"Yay!" cheered Ruby, scrambling up the ladder and arranging her cuddly toys on the top bunk.

"Ahoy there!" came a voice from outside the cottage, followed by a knock on the door.

Peggy and the girls hurried out to see who it was. A grizzled man with wild white hair stood on the doorstep, wearing wellie boots and a thick jumper, its sleeves pushed up to reveal a mermaid tattoo on his arm.

"You must be Captain Pete," said Dad, shaking his hand.

"Sorry I wasn't here when you got in," said Pete. "I was out on my boat." He held up a glistening silver fish. "I brought you a welcome gift."

"Oh, wow!" said Finn, impressed. "Did

you really catch that yourself?"

"Aye," said Pete, nodding.

As Dad put the fish in the refrigerator, Mum introduced everyone, including Peggy.

Captain Pete whistled and a huge dog bounded up from the beach. He had shaggy black fur and a red bandana tied around his neck. "This here is my first mate, Neptune."

Peggy had never seen such a big dog before. Neptune towered over her. "Hi," she said, wagging her curly tail to be friendly. "Are you named after the planet?" she said, remembering what Chloe had said about her science project.

"No," said Neptune, looking down at her. "I'm named after the god of the sea."

"Oh," said Peggy, feeling a bit silly. "Maybe we could play on the beach together tomorrow," she suggested.

Neptune shook his head. "I can't, I'm afraid. Not all of us are on holiday, you know," he said. "I'm a working dog –

I go out fishing with Captain Pete."

Now Peggy felt even sillier.

"Did you have any questions about the cottage?" asked Pete. "The plumbing can be a bit temperamental. Sometimes you need to jiggle the toilet handle when you flush it."

"I've got a question," Chloe said. "Have you ever seen a mermaid?"

The fisherman's eyes twinkled merrily. "Oh, aye," he said. "Lots of them. Why else do you think I named this place Mermaid Cottage?"

Ruby's eyes lit up and she clapped her hands in delight.

"I knew it!" said Chloe. She poked her

brother in the ribs. "Told you so."

"What about sharks?" Finn asked. "When you're out at sea do you see a lot of those too?"

Peggy hoped not!

But Pete reached into the neck of his sweater and pulled out a necklace made from a leather thong with a big, white tooth hanging from it. "I caught this one myself."

Finn whistled under his breath. "That is so cool," he said.

Ruby clutched Mum's hand, looking as scared as Peggy felt.

"Don't worry," said the fisherman, winking at her. "The bay is perfectly safe for swimming. I'll let you folks get settled in," he said, whistling to Neptune and ambling over to the other cottage.

After everyone had unpacked, Dad fired up the barbecue and grilled the fish Pete had brought them over the coals. When it was cooked, they ate dinner outside, watching the sun set. It sank down towards the horizon like a ball of flames, making the water glow with orange light.

"This is the life," said Mum, sitting back in her deckchair and sighing contentedly.

"I really like it here," said Chloe, smiling at her mother.

Me too, thought Peggy happily. She gobbled up her last bit of grilled fish and licked her chops. So far, being on holiday was amazing!

Chapter Four

"Wake up! We're on holiday!"

Peggy, who was curled up next to Chloe, opened her eyes and saw Ruby's grinning face hanging down from the top bunk. Chloe sat up so quickly she nearly bumped her head on the bed above. From the pale light streaming through the curtains, Peggy could tell it was still very early in the morning. But there was no time to waste – there was a beach to explore!

The girls jumped out of bed and quickly got dressed in their swimming costumes. They hurried into the kitchen, where Finn and Dad were eating cereal at the little table.

"We want to go to the beach," said Chloe.

"Breakfast first," said Dad.

The girls bolted down their cereal while Finn poured some dry dog food into a bowl for Peggy.

"Let's go!" shouted Ruby, when they'd

finished eating and done the washing up.

Dad pressed a finger to his lips. "Shh! Mum's having a lie-in," he said. "But I'll take you down to the beach."

Gathering up buckets and spades, towels and beach chairs, they left the cottage and headed down the dune-lined path to the beach. Peggy's short legs sank into the soft, golden sand as they walked towards the water. It was low tide, so the waves lapping at the sand were gentle.

Because it was early, the beach was still empty. They set out their towels and chairs, then they all ran down to the water's edge.

"There's Captain Pete!" said Finn,

waving to a fishing boat out in the bay. Neptune stood at the prow, looking very important.

Peggy barked hello to him, but either he didn't hear it over the noise of the boat – or he was just ignoring her.

"Let's look for shells," said Chloe, running along the beach.

"This one's pretty," said Ruby, picking up a fanned shell and adding it to her bucket.

"That's a cockle shell," said Dad.

The children found all sorts of empty shells – oysters, limpets, long razor clams, and spiral-shaped whelks. Soon their bucket was nearly full.

"We're never going to be able to take all of these home," chuckled Dad.

Peggy saw something black on the sand and gave it an inquisitive sniff. At first she thought it was a big bug, but it wasn't moving. She barked and everyone came running over.

"Peggy found a mermaid's purse,"
said Dad.

"Really?" said Chloe, picking it up
and studying it excitedly. "There must be
mermaids around here if one of them left
her handbag behind."

Dad laughed and shook his head. "A
mermaid's purse is actually a pouch
for shark eggs. This one's all dried out
though."

"Ugh," said Chloe, looking
disappointed.

Sharks? thought Peggy, glancing out at
the waves nervously.

"Cool!" said Finn, taking the
mermaid's purse off Chloe.

Wandering further along the beach, they came to some shallow rock pools, surrounded by rocks covered in barnacles and seaweed.

"Let's see if we can find any crabs," said Finn.

The children waded into the water and crouched down, peering among the rocks and slippery strands of seaweed.

Peggy noticed something moving behind a rock. Curious, she dipped her paw in the water and nudged the rock then— *SNAP!* Something pinched her paw!

"Ouch!" yelped Peggy.

"Do you mind?" snapped a crab,

staring at her with
bulging eyes.
"This is my
home."

"Sorry," said
Peggy, scurrying
away. So far, sea
creatures didn't seem
very friendly!

The children brought their buckets of
shells back to their towels. By now, the
sun had risen high in the clear, blue sky.
The tide was beginning to come in and
the beach had filled with other families.

"I'm hot," said Chloe. "Let's go
swimming. That will cool us off."

"Last one in's a rotten egg!" cried Finn, pulling off his T-shirt. He sprinted down to the water and dived straight in.

Chloe and Ruby held hands and ran, squealing, into the foamy, white waves. As Chloe floated on her back, riding the waves, Ruby paddled through the water proudly.

"Look, Daddy!" she called over to Dad, who had waded in up to his knees. "I'm swimming all on my own."

"Don't go out too deep, Rubes," he warned her.

"Come on in, Peggy," shouted Chloe. "The water's lovely!"

Peggy longed to play with the children,

but she was too scared to go in. The
waves were very big now. And there
might be crabs – or worse, *sharks* – in the
sea. Standing at the edge of the water,
Peggy watched Chloe, Finn and Ruby
splashing about. She kept her eyes peeled
for a mermaid. She knew how badly
Chloe wanted to see one.

A seagull waddled over to Peggy. "Hey, there, Four Legs," she squawked. "Watcha lookin' for?"

"A mermaid," said Peggy. "Do you know where I could find one?"

"Can't say I've seen any recently," said the seagull. "But I can tell you a good joke: Why did the mermaid blush?"

"Um, I'm not sure," said Peggy.

"Because the sea *weed*," cackled the seagull, flapping her wings in amusement. "Get it? I'm Pearl, by the way," she said.

"I'm Peggy," said Peggy, glad to have someone to talk to.

As Pearl pecked at the sand, searching for food, she told Peggy more jokes. "Why did the fish cross the ocean?" Pearl didn't even bother waiting for a reply. "To get to the other *tide*." She let out a loud squawk of laughter.

At lunchtime, Mum wandered down to the beach with a picnic hamper. The children came running out of the water, dripping wet. Wrapping themselves up in fluffy towels, they flopped down on the picnic blanket. Peggy came over to join them.

"I'm starving," said Chloe.

"Me too," said Finn.

"It must be the sea air," said Mum, handing out sandwiches, crisps and apples.

"Mmm," said Pearl, eyeing the picnic hungrily. "That sure looks good."

Chloe threw a few crisps to Peggy's new friend. Pearl gobbled them up, before any other seagulls could swoop down and get them.

"Don't encourage them," scolded Mum,

shooing the gull away with her hands. She took out a bottle of lotion from her bag. "Everyone needs to put on more sun cream."

"Yuck, it feels cold," said Ruby, squirming as Mum rubbed the lotion on to her back. A drop fell on Peggy's nose. It smelled like coconut.

"You've got to put it on, Rubes," said Mum. "Otherwise your skin will burn."

Mum put some on Chloe next, but when she tried to put some on Finn, he pulled away. "I'm not a baby – I can do it myself."

"Can I go swimming again?" asked Chloe, as soon as she'd finished eating.

"Not yet," said Mum. "You need to digest your food."

"What are we going to do if we can't go swimming?" said Chloe.

"When I walked down to the beach I noticed a sign for a sand sculpture competition," said Mum.

"Ooh! Let's enter it!" said Ruby.

"What should we make?" asked Dad.

"A shark," said Finn.

"They're making a shark already," said Mum, pointing to a family further down the beach who had started making a Great White out of sand.

"I've got an idea," said Chloe. "Let's make a mermaid!"

The whole family got to work. Peggy wanted to help, too, so she dug through the sand with her paws. Sand flew everywhere!

"Er, thanks, Peggy," laughed Chloe, shaking sand out of her hair.

They started shaping the mermaid's body. Dad and the girls worked on the mermaid's long tail, patting the damp sand into place with their hands, while Mum and Finn made her head, arms and tummy.

"We can use seaweed for her hair," said Chloe. Peggy ran along the beach, picking up long, slimy strands of seaweed in her mouth and bringing them back,

for Chloe to drape on the mermaid's
head.

"Let's decorate her with pretty pebbles
and the shells we found this morning,"

said Ruby, lugging her bucket of shells over.

As her family added shells to the mermaid's tail, Peggy wandered down the beach, checking out the competition. The team who had made the shark had used white pebbles for teeth. Even though she knew it wasn't real, Peggy couldn't help shivering. One family had made a huge sandcastle that looked like something from a fairy tale. It had four pointy turrets and a drawbridge made of ice lolly sticks. Another group had built a gigantic octopus and others had made a pirate ship, using an empty crisp packet for a flag.

All the sculptures were really good, but Peggy thought her family's mermaid was by far the best.

When she got back, the sand mermaid was holding the mermaid's purse they'd found that morning like a handbag. Her tail was covered in shells, making it look like she really had scales.

"Quick, we need to finish soon," said Mum, checking her watch. "The competition ends at four o'clock."

The judge walked up and down the beach holding a clipboard. He inspected all of the sand sculptures, jotting down notes. Then everyone gathered around as he announced the results.

"This was a really difficult decision," said the judge. "All of the sand sculptures are wonderful. But first prize goes to . . . the mermaid!"

Everyone clapped as Chloe and her family collected their prize – a blue rosette and a gift voucher to the local mini-golf course. Peggy barked happily over the applause. She was so proud of her family!

"We did it, Peggy!" Chloe said, attaching the rosette to her collar.

Then Dad asked the judge to take a photo of the whole family posing with the sand mermaid.

"What a perfect day," said Mum, as they started to gather up their beach things.

Chloe nodded as she folded up a beach chair. "The only thing that could have made it even better is seeing a *real* mermaid!"

I'll find one for you, thought Peggy.

They still had six more days of holiday – and she would keep looking until she found a mermaid for Chloe. There was nothing she wouldn't do to make her best friend happy!

Chapter Five

"Muuuuuum!" wailed Finn the next morning.

Peggy, Chloe and Ruby ran out of their bedroom to see what was wrong.

Finn stood in the kitchen wearing just his pyjama bottoms. His face, chest, arms and back were bright pink.

"Oh dear," said Mum. "You must not have put on enough sun cream yesterday. You've got sunburned."

"You look like a tomato," giggled Chloe.

"Your nose is red like a clown's," said Ruby, pointing as Finn glowered at them.

"Girls, that's not very nice," said Dad.

Mum found some soothing aloe lotion to put on Finn's sunburnt skin. He winced as she spread it on. Peggy felt glad she didn't need to worry about sunburn, thanks to her fur. It looked very painful!

"We'd better stay off the beach today,"

Mum said. "We can explore the harbour instead."

After breakfast, Dad drove everyone into the village centre. The cobbled streets were lined with quaint tea rooms, souvenir shops and fish-and-chip shops. The delicious smells wafting out of them made Peggy's tummy rumble.

They wandered over to the crescent-shaped harbour to look at the boats.

"Hey, there's Captain Pete," said Finn.

The fisherman waved to them from the pier, where he was unloading his catch. Neptune helped him drag nets full of glistening fish on to the dock.

"Need any help?" Peggy barked.

The big black dog looked up at her
and shook his head. "No thanks. I've got
this."

Peggy sighed. Neptune was helping
his owner with a very important job.
She wanted to be helpful, too. Then
she remembered what Chloe had said
yesterday. She *did* have a job – finding a
mermaid for Chloe.

A man in a pirate costume stood by
the harbour wall, ringing a bell. "Hear
ye! Hear ye!" he called. "There's a
free storytelling session starting in five
minutes."

"Ooh! That sounds great," said Mum,
herding everyone over to where a small

audience was beginning to form.

The pirate stood on a wooden crate, cleared his throat and adjusted his tri-corn hat. Then he began his story. "Today I'm going to tell you a local legend. It's about a sailor and . . ." he paused dramatically . . . "a mermaid!"

Finn groaned, but Chloe and Ruby exchanged excited looks.

Peggy cocked her ears and listened to the story, about a sailor who heard beautiful singing coming from the beach at night. He discovered the singer was a mermaid sitting on a rock, just off the shore.

The audience listened, captivated, as

the storyteller described the mermaid. "She had glittering silver scales that reflected the moonlight, long green hair with rippling waves and a voice as sweet as a choir of angels . . ."

"She sounds beautiful," Chloe
whispered to Ruby.

The storyteller told them how the
sailor fell in love with the mermaid and
followed her out to sea. He was never
seen in the village again. When the
storyteller finished speaking, everyone
applauded.

"I wonder what happened to the
sailor?" said Chloe, as they walked
over to the mini-golf course along the
seafront.

"He was probably eaten by a shark,"
said Finn, smirking.

"No he wasn't!" said Ruby. "The
mermaid took him to her underwater

palace and made him king of all the sea creatures."

At the mini-golf course, Dad handed over their voucher and everyone – apart from Peggy – got a golf club and a ball.

"This one matches your nose," Chloe said, handing Finn a red ball.

"Ha ha," he said. "Red's my lucky colour – I'm going to win."

The first hole had a lighthouse at the end of it. Chloe went first, tapping a blue ball with her club. The ball rolled down the green carpet and stopped just short of the hole.

"Aww!" said Chloe, disappointed. "It nearly went in."

Wanting to help, Peggy bounded forward and picked up the ball in her mouth.

"No, Peggy!" everyone cried.

Too late. Peggy dropped the ball right in the hole.

"Hole in one!" laughed Dad.

"That's cheating!" protested Finn.

"Naughty Peggy," scolded Chloe. "You mustn't move the balls."

Oops! Peggy felt bad. She'd just been trying to help.

As her family played golf, Peggy was careful not to touch the balls again – even though she was tempted to chase after them. Each hole had a different seaside theme – there were pirate ships and treasure chests and whales. Finally, they came to a hole with a big shark figure.

Peggy eyed it nervously, but it didn't move – even when Ruby accidentally whacked it with her golf club.

Finn tapped his red ball and it rolled through the shark's open jaws and plopped into the cup at the end. "Yes!" He danced around, celebrating his hole-in-one. "That puts me in the lead," he cheered.

When they got to the end of the course, a familiar seagull perched on top of the giant squid at the last hole. "Hey, Four Legs – how many tickles does it take to make an octopus laugh?" she squawked.

"Hi Pearl," Peggy said to her friend from the beach. She counted the octopus' legs and guessed the answer. "Is it eight?"

"No – ten tickles. *Tentacles*, get it?" The

seagull hopped up and down, laughing, then she asked, "Hey – are you still looking for a mermaid?"

"Yes," said Peggy.

"I've just seen one," said Pearl. "On the high street."

Peggy barked and tugged on her lead eagerly. "Come on!" she told Chloe. "We need to go – NOW!"

"I guess Peggy's had enough mini golf," chuckled Dad.

Peggy pranced impatiently as her family finished up their game and handed back their golf clubs. When they were back on the promenade, Peggy looked around. Where was the mermaid?

"She's over there!" squawked Pearl, gesturing with her wing as she circled overhead.

In the distance, Peggy saw something shiny glittering in the sun – the mermaid's tail!

Peggy tugged so hard on her lead that Chloe lost her grip. Her lead dragging behind her, Peggy raced down the street, as fast as her little legs could go.

Every so often, the mermaid stopped and handed a piece of paper to someone walking past. Panting hard, Peggy finally caught up with her, just outside a souvenir shop.

"Gotcha!" she said, biting the mermaid's tail to stop her from getting away.

"Whoa!" cried the mermaid. Her arms windmilled around wildly as she lost her balance and knocked over a display of beach balls. The balls bounced all over the street as the mermaid landed on her bottom. The pieces of paper she was holding flew through the air and fluttered down on to the cobblestones.

One of them landed next to Peggy – it had a picture of an ice cream cone on it.

"Peggy!" shouted Chloe, running over and picking her up. "What's got into you today?"

"I'm so sorry," said Dad, helping the mermaid up to her feet.

Huh? thought Peggy, confused. *Mermaids don't have feet . . .*

As the mermaid stood up and brushed herself off, Peggy realised that she hadn't found a mermaid. She'd found someone dressed up as a mermaid.

"I guess your dog really wants an ice cream," said the mermaid, smiling. She handed Dad one of her pieces of paper.

"The Frosty Mermaid," he said, reading the leaflet out loud.

"This coupon gets you a discount on ice creams," said the mermaid. She pointed to a shop a bit further down the road. "It's just there."

"Ooh! Can we get one?" asked Ruby.

"Not now," said Mum. "You'll spoil your lunch."

Chloe, Finn and Ruby helped the lady in the mermaid costume gather up all her leaflets, while Mum and Dad collected the brightly coloured beach balls, putting them back in a wire bin outside the souvenir shop. Peggy tried to help too, but the balls kept rolling away.

"Sorry again," said Dad.

"No harm done," said the mermaid lady, patting Peggy on the head. "Do pop in for an ice cream sometime."

"Can we go in the shop?" said Chloe, peering into the window.

"I suppose it's the least we can do," Mum said. "But you'd better keep hold of Peggy so she can't knock anything else over."

Peggy felt so ashamed. She thought she'd found a mermaid for Chloe, but instead she'd just made a mess.

The children had taken their pocket money on holiday, and they spent ages browsing in the souvenir shop. It

wasn't very big, but it was crammed
with postcards, sticks of rock, windmills,
colourful beach toys and trinkets made
from seashells.

Mum chose a pair of sunglasses with
mirrored lenses.

"Very cool," said Dad, winking at her
as he tried on a straw sunhat.

Finn picked out a fishing net for
himself and a rubber shaped like a shark
for his friend Zach.

"I just can't decide which one," said
Ruby, struggling to choose between
an inflatable swimming ring that looked
like a doughnut with pink sprinkles and
a float shaped like an ice lolly.

But Chloe didn't have any trouble deciding. She knew exactly what she wanted – a silver necklace with a charm shaped like a mermaid.

When Ruby finally decided on the inflatable doughnut, they paid for their purchases and left the shop.

Outside, Mum helped Chloe put her new necklace on straight away.

"It's so pretty," Chloe said, looking down at the little mermaid sparkling around her neck.

But Peggy knew it was a *real* mermaid that Chloe wanted. If she couldn't find one, there was no other option – she would just have to become a mermaid herself!

Chapter Six

That night, after dinner, Dad got out a deck of cards and started to shuffle them. "What game should we play?" he asked the others.

"How about rummy?" said Finn.

"That's too hard!" said Ruby. "Let's play Snap."

"I've got a better idea," said Chloe. "We're at the seaside – let's play Go Fish!"

As her family played card games, Peggy tried to work out how she was going to become a mermaid. In the film *The Little Mermaid*, a sea witch had used magic to make the mermaid a human. Maybe a sea witch could also turn a pug into a mermaid? Peggy shuddered. Sea witches were scary – there had to be a better way!

She suddenly remembered the story she'd heard at the harbour. The storyteller had said that mermaids sang at night. A plan began to form in Peggy's head. *I'll wait until everyone is asleep*, she decided, *and then I'll become a mermaid!*

Peggy glanced over at her family, wondering if they were nearly ready for bed. Ruby yawned and rested her head on the table. Peggy felt sleepy too – it had been a busy day. But she knew she needed to stay awake.

"I win!" announced Chloe, slapping her cards down on the table.

"Well done," said Mum, giving her a high five. "Let's tidy up now. It's bedtime."

"Awww," said Chloe. "But we're on holiday."

"Yeah," said Finn. "I want a rematch."

"We can play again tomorrow," said

Dad, picking up Ruby and carrying her into the girls' bedroom, as Mum gathered up the cards.

After Chloe had brushed her teeth and changed into her pyjamas, she climbed into the bottom bunk. "Sweet dreams, Peggy," she said, giving her a kiss goodnight. Then she rolled over and closed her eyes.

Peggy listened to Chloe's breathing become slow and steady, and soon she could tell her friend was fast asleep. Straining her ears, Peggy heard Dad gargling in the bathroom and Mum turning the pages of her book in the next room. Eventually, she heard the sound she was waiting for – *CLICK!* – as Mum and Dad turned off their bedroom light.

Peggy waited a while longer, until she was sure everyone was asleep, then she hopped down from Chloe's bed and padded out into the hall.

Mermaid Cottage was dark and silent, apart from Dad's snoring coming from the grown-ups' bedroom. When she got to the front door, Peggy hesitated. It was very dark outside – what if she got lost and fell in the sea and was eaten by a shark? For a moment, Peggy wanted to crawl back into bed and snuggle up with Chloe.

You're doing this for her, she reminded herself. Peggy owed so much to Chloe, who loved and cared for her. Now it was Peggy's turn to help her friend. Chloe really wanted to see a mermaid, so Peggy needed to make that happen.

She nudged the door open with her paw but it was locked. Luckily, the living room window was open a bit to let in the cool night air. Peggy climbed up on a chair and squeezed through the gap. Then she jumped down, her paws landing on soft sand. She was outside!

Oh wow! she thought, staring up in amazement.

Back at home, there weren't nearly so many stars in the night sky. Here, away from the city lights, the inky black sky sparkled with tiny pinpricks of light. Peggy thought about Chloe's solar system project – it was hard to believe that way up in the universe, there were enormous planets, too. As she looked up, a comet blazed across the sky, leaving a glittering trail of white behind it. Peggy saw another shooting star – and another!

Peggy's fur stood on end as she watched the stars dance like fireworks across the sky. Tonight, there was magic in the air. Anything felt possible – even a pug becoming a mermaid!

Once her eyes had adjusted to the dark, Peggy got to work. She hurried down to the beach and found some slimy strands of seaweed and draped them over her head. There! Now she had long, green hair.

But mermaids also had tails . . .

Peggy looked around, looking for something to use as a tail. Outside Captain Pete's cottage, there was a jumble of fishing nets.

Aha! thought Peggy. Those would be perfect!

She dragged one of the nets over with her teeth and arranged it around her hind legs like a tail. Now that she looked like a mermaid, it was time to sing. Taking a deep breath, Peggy began to howl. *AROOOOOOOO! ARRRRROOOOOOOOOO! ARRRRRRRRROOOOOOOOOO!*

Lights switched on in Mermaid Cottage, and then in the fisherman's cottage next door. Peggy sang her heart out, hoping she sounded as beautiful as the mermaid in the story.

One by one, Peggy's family stumbled

outside in their
pyjamas. Captain
Pete came out
in his dressing
gown, too, with
Neptune by his
side.

"Peggy?" said
Chloe, squinting at
her through the dark.

Peggy's heart sank. Chloe didn't think
she was a mermaid. She'd recognised her
straight away.

"Oh, you poor thing," said Chloe,
scooping her up. She picked the seaweed
off Peggy's head and threw it on the

ground. "Ugh!" she said. "That stinks."

"I'm so sorry she woke you up," Mum apologised to Captain Pete. "I have no idea how she got out."

"She must have got tangled up in one of your fishing nets," said Dad, returning the net to Pete.

"No worries," said Pete, chuckling. "I'm glad she's OK. When I heard all that howling, I thought she'd injured herself."

They all went back inside the cottage. Peggy tried to climb on to Chloe's bed but Mum shooed her out of the bedroom. "You're sleeping on the floor tonight, Peggy," she said, shutting the door. "You smell terrible."

Curled up on the hard floor, Peggy felt ashamed. She'd woken everybody up in the middle of the night – and all for nothing. If she couldn't become a mermaid on a magical night like tonight, when *could* she?

After breakfast the next morning, they trooped down to the beach. While Dad set out the blankets and parasol, Mum spread sun cream on everyone. This time Finn didn't protest. As Mum and Dad settled down in the parasol's shade to read their books, Peggy looked around for someone to play with.

She tried Finn first, nudging him with her paw. "Sorry, Peggy," he said, putting on his headphones. "I'm just not in the mood to play."

Next, Peggy went over to Ruby, who was lying on a beach towel, her eyes shut. Peggy licked her cheek and Ruby opened one eye. "I'm taking a nap," she murmured sleepily.

Peggy went over to Chloe and tugged on her swimming costume playfully. Chloe looked up from the text message she was writing and shook her head. "Maybe later, Peggy," she said. "I'm sending a message to Hannah – she says Coco is doing well."

Dejected, Peggy wandered down to the water and stared out at the sea. Nobody wanted to play with her – and she only had herself to blame. It was all her fault everyone was so tired. She had to make it up to them somehow. Maybe she could still find a mermaid. But there was only one place she hadn't looked so far – in the water.

Gathering her courage, Peggy waded into the sea, her paws sinking into the sand as water swirled around her short legs. She went in a bit deeper, until the water reached up to her tummy. *Brrr!* It was a bit chilly. A big wave swelled in the distance. It curled and came rushing towards the beach. Crashing over Peggy's head, it knocked her off her paws and dragged her underwater.

Salty water stung Peggy's eyes and went up her nose. She kicked her paws frantically, trying to fight her way back to the beach. But the waves were much too strong. They kept sucking her down, under the water's surface!

"Help!" Peggy yelped, swallowing a mouthful of water. She felt herself being pulled further and further away from the beach by the tide.

Then, out of nowhere, something picked her up by the scruff of her neck, the way her mum had carried her when

she was a puppy. A moment later, it set
her down gently on the warm sand.
Peggy looked up and saw her saviour –
Neptune.

The big dog towered over her, looking
cross. "What were you trying to do?" he
growled. "Drown?"

"No!" she spluttered. "I was trying to find a mermaid."

"A mermaid, eh?" Understanding flickered in Neptune's wise brown eyes. "Is that what last night was all about too?" he asked her.

Peggy nodded sheepishly. "Chloe loves mermaids," she explained. "Last night I tried to become a mermaid, but when that didn't work I decided I needed to find one for her in the water. You probably think I'm stupid, right?"

Neptune shook his head sympathetically. "You were just trying to help your friend. I'd do anything for Captain Pete, too. But you shouldn't go into the water if you don't know how to swim."

Peggy sighed. "I guess I'll never find a mermaid for Chloe now."

"Look," said Neptune. "I don't know anything about finding mermaids. But I *can* teach you how to swim."

"Really?" asked Peggy.

"Of course," said Neptune. "Ever heard of the doggy paddle? They named it after us for a reason."

Peggy looked out at the sea anxiously. The waves were VERY big. What if they pulled her under again – she might get swept out to sea, where a shark could eat her. She would never see Chloe again . . .

"I'll keep you safe," promised Neptune. "I'm a Newfoundland dog. We've got waterproof fur and special webbed paws to help us swim." He held up his front paw to show her. "That's why fishermen take us out on their boats – because we're lifesavers."

"That's really cool," said Peggy.

"Come on," said Neptune. "Let's get started."

First, Peggy needed to get used to getting her face wet. "Good girl," Neptune said as she lowered her face into the foamy waves.

"That tickles," giggled Peggy.

When she was ready, they went out a

bit deeper. "Don't worry, I've got you," Neptune said. Peggy used her teeth to hold on to his shaggy fur as he towed her through the water. "Kick your back paws," he coached her. Peggy did what he said. "Now your front paws . . . and . . . let go," said Neptune.

Peggy felt scared, but she let go of Neptune's fur and paddled her legs furiously. Instead of sinking, she was swimming!

Peggy paddled up and down the beach, holding her head above the waves. "I can do it!" she yipped happily. "I can doggy paddle!"

"Well done!" barked Neptune.

"Way to go, Peggy!" called Pearl, flying overhead.

The barking and squawking attracted everyone's attention.

"Look!" cried Chloe, running down to the water with Finn and Ruby following close behind her. "Peggy's swimming!"

The children ran into the water, and soon they were all splashing and playing in the waves. Peggy couldn't believe she'd been too scared to go in the sea before. Swimming was so much fun!

Ruby blew bubbles in the water and Peggy chased after them, popping them with her paws.

"I'm so proud of you," said Chloe, stroking Peggy's damp head.

"I'll leave you to it," said Neptune, getting out of the water and shaking himself off. Water glistened on his thick, black fur.

"Thank you so much," said Peggy, her

big eyes shining with gratitude. "You saved my life."

"I was just doing my job," said Neptune, winking. "Good luck finding a mermaid."

But Peggy had found something even more exciting than a mermaid – a hero!

Chapter Seven

Over the next few days, Peggy had lots
of fun playing in the sea with Chloe,
Ruby and Finn. She loved being in the
water now! They jumped over waves,
had swimming races and floated on
Ruby's inflatable ring. No matter
what they were doing, Peggy always

kept a lookout for the silvery flash of a mermaid's tail. She saw plenty of little fish and once she even spotted a seal stick his whiskered face out of the water, but she still hadn't seen a mermaid.

On the last day of their holiday, Peggy stood on the sand, gentle waves lapping at her paws, and stared out at the coast. *I've got to find a mermaid for Chloe,* she thought. Time was running out – they were going home tomorrow!

A seagull swooped down and landed next to Peggy. "What's wrong, Four Legs?" Pearl squawked.

"I'm looking for a mermaid," said Peggy, peering into the distance.

"Still? I thought I found one for you in town," said Pearl.

Peggy shook her head sadly. "She wasn't a real mermaid," she told the seagull. "Just someone dressed up in a costume."

"That's a shame," said Pearl. "But I've got a new joke that might cheer you up – what did the sea say to the sand?"

Peggy looked down at the damp sand. "Er—"

"Nothing!" squawked Pearl. "It just WAVED!"

But Pearl's joke didn't make Peggy feel better. She turned and looked at Chloe, who was building a sandcastle with Ruby further up the beach. The thing her friend wanted most from this holiday was to see a mermaid. Peggy had promised to help her find one, but she had failed.

"The beach is pretty crowded at this time of year," said Pearl, eyeing up a toddler holding a tuna sandwich. "Mermaids are shy. They're probably keeping well away."

Of course! thought Peggy. The beach was full of families swimming, sunbathing and enjoying picnics. No wonder they hadn't seen a mermaid!

The little boy dropped his sandwich on the ground. "Gotta go!" said Pearl.

The seagull swooped over, snatched the sandwich with her beak, and flew away with her prize.

Peggy gazed out at the sea, which seemed to stretch endlessly into the distance. Mermaids were somewhere way out there. But how could she get to them? She was a good swimmer now, but her short legs could only doggy paddle so far . . .

Just then, Chloe ran up to Peggy. "Guess what?" she cried. "Captain Pete has invited us to go fishing on his boat!"

Peggy let out an excited bark. This was perfect – a boat would take her far out to sea where she could find a mermaid!

Wagging her tail, she hurried back to the others with Chloe.

Pete's boat was tied to a buoy at the far end of the beach, bobbing in the shallows. Neptune was already on board, keeping lookout by the prow. He barked in greeting when he saw them wading towards the boat.

"Welcome aboard!" said Pete, reaching down to help them climb into the boat. Chloe passed Peggy up to the captain, then hauled herself on to the deck.

"I'm going to catch the biggest fish," boasted Finn.

"No, I am!" said Chloe.

Peggy didn't care about catching fish

– she just wanted to catch sight of a mermaid!

Captain Pete handed out life jackets to everyone.

"I don't need one of these," said Ruby. "I know how to swim."

"Everyone needs to wear one," said Pete firmly. "I don't want Neptune to have to jump in and rescue you."

Peggy knew they'd all be safe with Neptune to look after them, but she was glad to see Ruby put on her life jacket. Pete raised the anchor, switched on the engine and the boat chugged out to sea. Peggy rested her paws on the side of the boat, enjoying the feel of sea spray on

her furry face. She watched as the people
on the beach grew smaller and smaller.
Eventually, they disappeared from view
completely.

As they went into deeper water, the
wind picked up. The fishing boat rocked
on the waves and Peggy's tummy began

to churn. She wasn't the only one feeling seasick – Dad and Ruby both looked a bit green as they gripped the railing.

"Ugggggghhhhh!" Peggy moaned, staggering around the deck queasily.

"Don't worry," chuckled Neptune. "You'll soon find your sea legs."

Peggy collapsed on a pile of fishing nets and closed her eyes. But Neptune was right – it didn't take long to get used to the rocking motion.

By the time Captain Pete switched off the engine, Peggy's stomach had settled.

"What do you think, Neptune?" asked Pete. "Does this look like a good spot?"

Neptune barked his approval.

Captain Pete dropped the anchor, then he handed out fishing rods to his guests and taught them how to cast their line.

"Oops!" giggled Chloe as she accidentally hooked Dad's shorts. "Told you I was going to catch a big one."

"You won't catch anything without some bait," said Pete. He opened up his tackle box to reveal worms wriggling and squirming inside.

"Ew!" said Finn. Now HE looked a bit

green. "That's so gross."

"Don't be such a wimp," said Chloe, putting a worm on the end of her line.

As her family threw their fishing lines into the water and waited to see if anything bit, Peggy scanned the waves, looking for a mermaid. To her disappointment, the only things she could see were a few sailing boats in the distance and some seagulls bobbing on the waves.

"I think I've got a nibble!" shouted Chloe.

Captain Pete pressed a finger to his lips. "You need to be quiet or you'll scare all the fish away."

"Sorry!" whispered Chloe.

"OK, let's see what you've got," said Pete, helping Chloe reel in her fishing line. A small silver fish dangled from the end of it.

"We need to throw it back," said Pete, unhooking the fish and tossing it into the water.

"Why?" asked Chloe.

"It's just a tiddler," said Pete. "We only keep the big ones. It's important to let the little fish grow up. That way there will always be plenty of fish in the sea."

A while later, Ruby's line jerked. Something was tugging at the end of it!

"Help!" Ruby called, struggling to

keep hold of her fishing rod. Neptune hurried over and bit the bottom of her life jacket so she didn't go overboard.

"It must be a big one!" said Finn. He handed his fishing rod to Dad, and helped Ruby reel in her line.

"Easy does it," coached Pete.

Suddenly, there was a flash of silver, as Finn and Ruby pulled a huge sea bass out of the water.

"Oh wow!" said Finn. "It's massive!"

"Now this one is a keeper," said Pete.

"I thought it was going to pull me in the water!" said Ruby.

"I've got to get a picture of that," said Mum, taking out her phone. As Ruby and Finn posed proudly with their fish, its scales gleaming in the sunlight, something in the water caught Peggy's eye. She ran over to the side of the boat and peered over the railing. Could it really be . . . .?

A shimmering silver fin stuck out of the water. It was a mermaid's tail!

Peggy jumped up on Chloe's legs, trying to get her attention. "Look in the water!" she barked, hoping Chloe would notice the mermaid.

"Shh!" Chloe scolded her. "You'll scare the fish away."

"What's wrong?" Neptune asked Peggy.

"Nothing!" said Peggy. "I've just seen a mermaid!"

She ran back to the side of the boat, but the silver mermaid tail had disappeared under the water. *Oh no! Where has it gone?* Peggy looked around wildly, and then she spotted the silver fin slicing through the water. The mermaid was getting away!

"Come back!" she barked.

There was no time to lose – she had to stop the mermaid. Without even pausing to think, Peggy climbed over the side of the boat . . . and dived into the sea!

Chapter Eight

SPLASH! Peggy hit the water and sank down . . . down . . . down. The water was a lot colder and deeper this far out at sea! Kicking her legs, she swam up to the surface and gasped for breath.

"Hey wait!" she called, spotting the mermaid's silver tail fin in the distance.

She swam towards it, through the choppy waves.

To Peggy's relief, the fin turned and started moving towards her. As it got closer, a long, grey shape emerged from the water. Peggy gasped in terror. It wasn't a mermaid. It was a shark — and it was coming for her!

"Help!" howled Peggy. "A shark is going to eat me!"

A face with beady eyes and a pointed nose popped out of the water and regarded Peggy with amusement. "Who are you calling a shark?" she said, laughing. "I'm a dolphin."

"Are you going to eat me?" Peggy

asked nervously. The dolphin seemed friendly, but when she opened her mouth, Peggy saw sharp white teeth.

"That depends," teased the dolphin in a squeaky voice. "What kind of fish are you?"

"I'm not a fish," said Peggy. "I'm a pug. My name's Peggy."

"I'm Misty," said the dolphin. "Don't

worry, I'm not going to eat you – you're much too furry!"

Peggy's relief at not being eaten soon turned to disappointment, as she realised she had jumped overboard for no reason. Blinking back tears, she turned and looked at the boat.

Chloe was leaning over the side, looking frantic with worry. "Dog overboard!" she cried, pointing at Peggy.

Captain Pete got a life ring and threw it into the water.

Neptune peered over the railing. "Need me to come and rescue you?" he barked down to Peggy.

"No, I'm fine," she called back. But her

legs were beginning to feel very tired from treading water. "I don't suppose you could give me a lift back to the boat?" she asked Misty.

"Of course," said the dolphin. "Hop on my back!"

Peggy scrambled on to the dolphin's slippery back and balanced like a surfer. "Whee!" she shouted in delight as the dolphin raced through the water.

"So did you fall overboard?" asked Misty.

"No, I jumped in," explained Peggy. "I was trying to find a mermaid for my friend Chloe. Do you know where I could find one?"

Misty shook her head. "Can't say I've ever seen one."

Peggy sighed. "It's our last day of holiday and I really wanted to make it special for Chloe."

Misty cocked her head to the side thoughtfully. "*Hmm* – my pod might be able to help with that . . ."

When they reached the life ring, Peggy clutched it with her paws and Captain Pete pulled her back up to the boat.

"This is definitely the catch of the day," said Captain Pete, chuckling. Peggy shook herself dry, splattering everyone with drops of water.

"Oh, Peggy," said Chloe, picking her

up and hugging her. "I was so scared I was going to lose you."

"That dolphin saved her," said Ruby, pointing at Misty.

Out in the water, the dolphin made some high-pitched whistling and clicking noises. A few minutes later, a whole pod of dolphins surrounded Misty, water glistening on their smooth, silver backs as their long mouths chattered excitedly.

"Look at all of them!" gasped Chloe.

"Listen up, everybody," Misty said to the other dolphins. She gestured towards the boat with her fin. "Let's give Peggy the pug and her friend Chloe a special show they'll never forget!"

The dolphins clicked and slapped their fins against the water. Then they all shot forward and jumped up high, their sleek bodies arcing above the sea. They raced through the waves, leaping again and again as they swam around the boat. Peggy and her family watched in awe as the dolphins did flips and twists in the air, graceful as ballet dancers. For their grand finale, the dolphins slapped the water with their tail fins, cheekily splashing the humans on the boat.

"The dolphins got me wet," giggled Ruby, wiping drops of water off her face.

"That was the coolest thing I've ever seen," said Finn with a huge grin.

"It was awesome," Chloe said breathlessly.

"How was that?" Misty called up to Peggy. "Special enough for you?"

"That was amazing," said Peggy. "Thank you so much!"

"No problem," said Misty, waving goodbye with her fin.

The dolphins swam off. Peggy and her family watched them leaping through the water until they'd vanished into the distance.

"Wow," said Chloe, cuddling Peggy tight. "Just . . . wow."

That evening, Dad grilled the fish Ruby had caught on the barbecue. It was so big, they invited Captain Pete and Neptune to join them for dinner. Even though she wasn't invited, Pearl came too, swooping down to gobble up any bits of food that fell on the ground.

As they sat outside, eating fish and corn on the cob, all anyone could talk about was the dolphins.

"In all my years at sea, I've never seen anything like that before," said Captain Pete, shaking his head.

"It was spectacular," said Mum.

"Unforgettable," agreed Dad.

Neptune and Peggy lay next to each

other, basking in the warm rays of the setting sun.

Pearl waddled over to the two dogs. "Hey – where do dolphins sleep?" she asked them.

"I know!" said Peggy, guessing the punch line. "On a sea bed!"

Cackling, the seagull hurried off to snatch a piece of fish Ruby had dropped on the ground.

"That was pretty impressive swimming today," said Neptune.

"Well," said Peggy modestly, "I had a good teacher."

"You could work on a fishing boat like me, if you wanted to," said Neptune.

Peggy felt flattered, but she knew she wasn't meant to be a sea dog like Neptune. "Thanks," she told her friend. "But I belong with my family."

Neptune nodded. "I can tell you love them very much," he said.

Oh, I do, thought Peggy, glancing over at Chloe.

"Who wants ice cream?" asked Dad.

"Me!" cried Chloe, Ruby and Finn.

Captain Pete and Neptune went home to bed because they had an early start the next morning, but Peggy and her family drove to the harbour. They stopped outside The Frosty Mermaid and went into the ice cream parlour.

There were so many flavours to choose from that it took ages to decide. In the end, Dad got pistachio, Mum got coffee, Ruby got strawberry and Finn chose one scoop of mint chocolate chip and one scoop of lemon sorbet.

"That sounds disgusting," said Chloe, wrinkling her nose.

"It's the best combination," said Finn, licking his cone.

Chloe ordered a cup of the house special, which had swirls of pink and purple, blue and green. It was called Mermaid Surprise.

When she had eaten half of it, Chloe set the cup on the ground. "I'm full.

You can have the rest, Peggy."

Mmmm! Peggy lapped up the melting ice cream. It tasted delicious!

"I wish we didn't have to go home tomorrow," said Finn, sighing.

"I know," said Ruby, nibbling the end of her cone. "It's so fun here."

"It has been a truly wonderful holiday," said Mum.

Chloe nodded. "I didn't get to see a mermaid," she said. "But thanks to Peggy, I got to see something even cooler – dolphins!"

Peggy's heart swelled with love and pride. She hadn't let her best friend down after all!

"Maybe we'll come here again next summer," said Dad. "What do you think?"

"Yes!" cried the kids.

"Yes!" barked Peggy.

Chloe picked her up and they all watched the sun setting over the beautiful harbour. Peggy snuggled in her friend's arms and sighed happily. Her first holiday had been amazing, and she couldn't wait to come back!

The End

Don't miss Peggy the pug's next adventure!

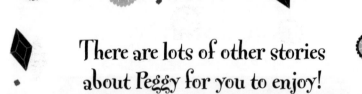

There are lots of other stories
about Peggy for you to enjoy!

The Pug who wanted to be a
Bunny

Bella Swift

The Pug who wanted to be a
Pumpkin

Bella Swift

Have you read all these great
animal stories by Bella Swift?